This book belongs to...

WILLIAM

trunk trouble

Written by Ronne Randall
Illustrated by Jacqueline East

Bright Sparks ☆

Emma, Ellen and Eric Elephant had spent nearly all day at the river, splashing and sploshing in the cool, clear water and giving each other excellent elephant showers.

But now it was nearly dinner time, and their rumbling tummies told them it was time to head for home.

First the little elephants had to dry themselves off.
They made their way out to the clearing, and carefully
dusted themselves with fine earth and sand.

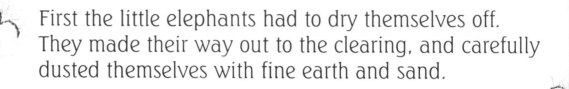

WHOOSH!   WHOOSH!

PUFFLE!

went Ellen with her trunk.

PUFFLE!   PUFFLE!   WHOOSH!

went Emma with her trunk.
Both sisters had long, graceful trunks,
and they were very proud of them.

WHOOSH! PUFFLE! WHOOSH... PUFF!

went Eric, when his
sisters' backs were turned.

"COUGH!" "COUGH!"

"AH-CHOO!"

went Emma and Ellen.
"Hey! Cut it out!" they
shouted.

Eric just giggled. He loved annoying his sisters.

"I'll race you home!" Eric called, when they were all dry. "Last one back is an elephant egg!" And he loped back into the jungle.

Ellen and Emma ran after him. "We'll get there first! We'll beat you!" they cried, going as quickly as they could.

Ellen and Emma were running so fast and trying so hard to catch up with their brother that they forgot to look where they were going.

All at once, Emma's feet got caught in a leafy, trailing vine, and she stumbled and lost her balance.

"Oh-oh-OOOOHHHH!" she cried as she slipped and staggered and started to fall.

"Grab my trunk!" Ellen cried, reaching out to her sister.

But Emma grabbed her sister's trunk so hard that she pulled Ellen down with her. As the two elephants struggled to straighten up, their trunks got twisted together in a great big tangle.

"Help!" they cried. "Eric! Help!"

When their brother turned and saw what had happened, he came bounding back.

"Don't worry!" he called. "I'll save you!"

Eric reached out with his trunk to try to help his sisters up. But the vine leaves were very slippery, and as he grabbed his sisters' trunks, he slipped and lost his balance, too. Now Eric's trunk was all tangled up with Emma's and Ellen's!

The three elephants sat there in a sad, tangled heap. They couldn't straighten out their trunks, they couldn't pull themselves apart – they could hardly even move.

"What are we going to do?" wailed Emma.

"Don't worry, someone will come and help us," Ellen said, trying to reassure her.

"This is all your fault!" Eric grumbled. "If it wasn't for you two, I'd be home by now, eating my dinner!"

A moment later, Seymour Snake came slithering by.

"Greetingssss," he hissed, looking curiously at the heap of elephants.

"Isss thisss an interesting new game?"

"It's not a game at all!" sobbed Emma. "We're all tangled together and we can't get up. Can you help us, Seymour?"

"Well I'll certainly do my bessst," said Seymour.

"Let's see if I can untwissst you."

He wriggled in amongst the tangle of trunks to see what he could do.

But everything was so muddled and jumbled together that Seymour couldn't even find his way out!

"Graciousss me!"

he exclaimed.

"I ssseem to be sssstuck!"

"Well, that's just great!" said Eric. "As if we didn't have enough problems – now we have a snake to worry about, too!"

"I ssssuggest you sssstart thinking about a ssssolution to all thissss," Seymour hissed.

Just then Mickey and Maxine Monkey came swinging through the branches.

"HEY, YOU GUYS!"

they shouted. They weren't very far away – Mickey and Maxine always shouted.

"WHAT'S GOING ON?"

"We're stuck!" cried Ellen. "Please help us get untangled so we can go home!"

"Well, we can try pulling you apart," said Maxine, scurrying down to inspect the pile of elephants and snake. "Mickey, you take a tail, and I'll take some ears."

Mickey grabbed hold of Eric's tail, and Maxine gripped Emma's ears. Then they both pulled and pulled and

p-u-l-l-e-d.

"OUCH!"
cried Eric.

"OUCH-OUCH-OOUUCCHH!"
bellowed Emma.

"I'm being ssssqueezzzzed breathlessssss!" hissed Seymour in alarm.

Mickey and Maxine gave up. Pulling clearly wasn't going to work.

Suddenly there was a flapping up above as Portia
Parrot and her daughter Penelope landed in a tree.
They had something in their beaks, and as everyone
looked up, they let it go. A large cloud of dry, dusty,
sandy earth drifted down.

"Cough-cough-ca-choooo!"

spluttered Mickey and Maxine.

"Cough-cough-ca-choooo!"

thundered the elephants.

For a moment, they didn't know what had happened.
Then they realised – they had sneezed themselves apart!

"Thank you," cried the elephants. "Thank you sssSoooo much!" exclaimed Seymour.

"It was Penelope's idea," said Portia.

"Everyone's invited to our house for dinner!" said Eric.

"Hooray!" cried the others.

With their trunks held high, the elephants led the way back to their house – walking calmly and slowly, and very, **very** carefully!

This is a Bright Sparks Book
First published in 2000
BRIGHT SPARKS, Queen Street House, 4 Queen Street, Bath BA1 1HE, UK

Copyright © PARRAGON 2000

Created and produced by THE COMPLETE WORKS,
St. Mary's Road, Royal Leamington Spa, Warwickshire CV31 1JP, UK

Editorial Director: Mike Phipps
Project Manager: Stuart Branch
Editor: Aneurin Rhys
Designer: Anne Matthews

ISBN 1-84250-037-6

Printed in China